A STEVEN SPIELBERG PRESENTATION
OF A DON BLUTH FILM

W9-BLR-087

An American Tail ™

Escape from the Catsacks

by **Michael Teitelbaum**

From a screenplay by **Judy Freudberg** & **Tony Geiss**
Based upon characters created by **David Kirschner**

Illustrations from the Don Bluth film

PlayValue Books®
A Division of Grosset & Dunlap

© 1986 Universal City Studios, Inc. and U-Drive Productions, Inc. All Rights Reserved. Published simultaneously in Canada. PlayValue Books is a registered trademark of The Putnam Publishing Group. Grosset & Dunlap is a member of The Putnam Publishing Group, New York. Printed in the U.S.A. ISBN 0-448-48614-8   A B C D E F G H I J

AMBLIN
ENTERTAINMENT

UNIVERSAL
PICTURES
An MCA Company

Once, long ago in the year 1885 in a small town in Russia, there lived a family of mice known as the Mousekewitzes. Like many of the other mice families living in their town, they were quite poor. Despite their poverty, the Mousekewitz family was filled with love, and was very content with the simple life they lived.

This evening was particularly special. It was Chanukah. Mama Mousekewitz made a delicious holiday dinner. After dinner she rocked baby Yasha in her lap, while Papa Mousekewitz played lively music on his violin. Their other children, Fievel and Tanya, danced and sang and played Chanukah games as they giggled with delight.

"When do we open our presents, Papa?" asked young Fievel with great excitement.

"Oh, yes, our presents," beamed his sister, Tanya.

"Presents?" teased Papa. "What presents?"

"Oh, Papa!" scolded Mama, gently. "Give them their presents, already." The whole family laughed at Papa's playful teasing.

"Oh, your Chanukah presents, you mean," smiled Papa, putting down his violin and reaching behind his back. "Here you go, Tanya." He handed his daughter a rolled-up scarf. The Russians called them "babushkas." This one was old and patched, but Tanya was still thrilled with the gift.

"Oh, Papa," cried Tanya, hugging her father. "A new babushka. Thank you, Papa. Thank you, Mama."

"What about me!" shouted Fievel, jumping up and down impatiently.

Papa reached up and took the old, but handsome hat off his head, and placed it on Fievel's. "For you, my son, this special hat. It has been in our family for three generations, and now I pass it on to you!"

The hat was too big for Fievel and it fell down over his eyes, but he beamed with pride as he looked at himself in a mirror. It was indeed the best Chanukah that any of them could remember.

"Tell us a story, Papa," said Fievel, lifting the hat up off his eyes.

"Yes, Papa, a story," added Tanya.

"Well—" started Papa.

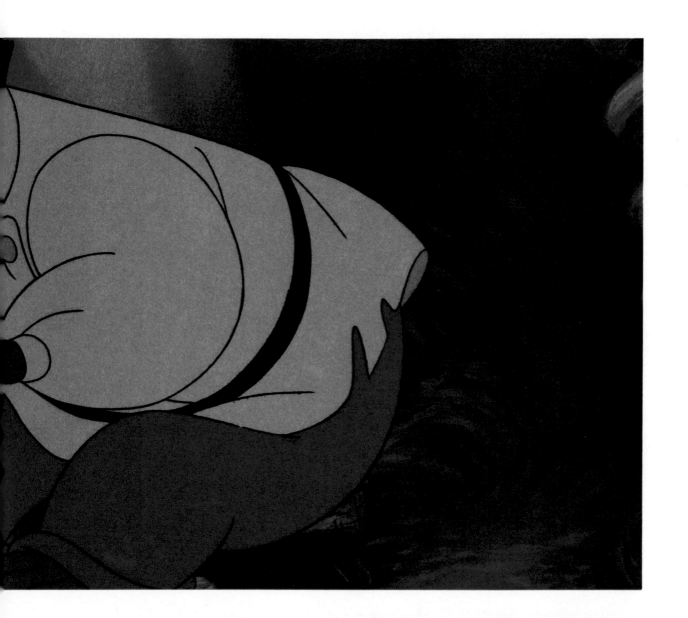

"Tell us about America!" interrupted Fievel, longing to
hear again about the magical land across the ocean.

Papa settled back into his chair. "In America," he began, "there are mouseholes in every wall!" His children looked up at him in wide-eyed amazement.

"In America," he continued, "there are bread crumbs on every floor! But best of all," Papa paused and looked around cautiously, "in America, there are no cats!"

"Shhh!" warned Mama. "They'll hear you!"

"Wow!" exclaimed Fievel. "No cats!"

Suddenly the room began to shake. The Mousekewitzes heard the thunder of hundreds of feet galloping into their town. It was a huge gang of cats known as the *Catsacks*, and they had stormed into town to destroy the quiet little village that so many mice called home.

Fievel thought he could scare the Catsacks away. He grabbed a large spoon and a pan from the kitchen and ran out into the snow.

"Fievel, come back!" shouted Mama, but it was too late.

Fievel charged at a Catsack, banging the spoon on the pan and shouting, "Go away, cats! Go away!" But the cats did not go away. They chased little Fievel right back into his house where Mama and Papa were preparing to leave.

The Catsacks continued to set fire to some of the mouse homes and demolish others with their razor-sharp claws. Entire families were captured by the Catsacks, others were driven out into the snow and left homeless. Their raid was swift, efficient, and totally devastating.

The Mousekewitzes acted quickly. They gathered up some of their prized possessions, such as Papa's violin, and fled their burning home. By the time the terrible Catsacks had gone, their house and most of their belongings had been completely destroyed.

Papa felt thankful that his family was still alive as he stared at the burnt ruins of his home.

"In America there are no cats," whispered Papa. "That is where we will go. America!"

His family looked up at him and each thought about the lives they were leaving behind, and the long journey and new life that lay ahead.

After several months on the road, the weary travelers finally arrived in the city of Hamburg, in Germany. There, a boat was waiting to carry them to America.

"Look, Papa, water!" shouted Fievel, as the Mousekewitzes climbed up the rope leading onto the boat. "Is that the ocean?"

"Yes, Fievel," answered Papa. "Keep walking!"

"Are those sea gulls, Papa," asked Fievel with uncontrollable curiosity, when he spotted two birds overhead.

"Just keep walking," came the reply.

Soon the Mousekewitzes were on board. There they met mice of many different nationalities. As the ship pulled away from the dock, hearts were filled with a little fear and much anticipation. Eyes welled up with tears as many gazed on their homeland for the last time.

"We're really going to America!" said Fievel, hugging Papa.

"America," sighed Mama, clutching Yasha and Tanya close to her.

It was true, the Mousekewitzes and their shipmates were headed, with high hopes, for the land of freedom and no cats—America!